Original Korean text by Cecil Kim
Illustrations by Mique Moriuchi

This English edition published by big & SMALL in 2016
by arrangement with Yeowon Media
English text edited by Joy Cowley

Distributed in the United States and Canada by
Lerner Publishing Group, Inc.
241 First Avenue North
Minneapolis, MN 55401 U.S.A.
www.lernerbooks.com

ISBN: 978-1-925248-61-6
Printed in Korea

Written by Cecil Kim
Illustrated by Mique Moriuchi
Edited by Joy Cowley

"Wake up, Annie!
It's time for school."

“Have fun with friends, Annie.”

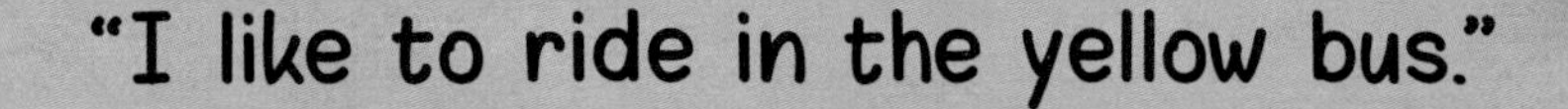

"I like to ride in the yellow bus."

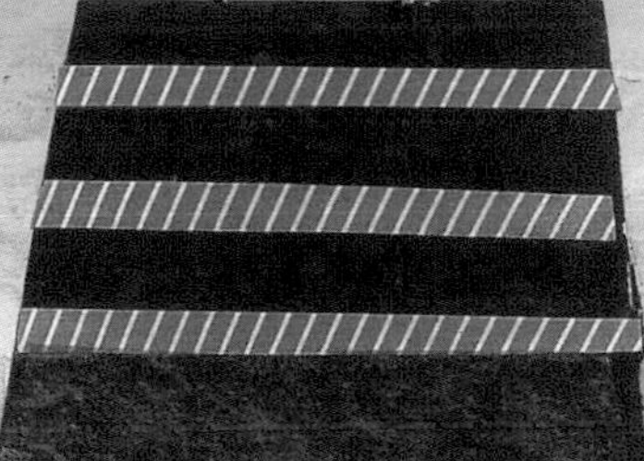

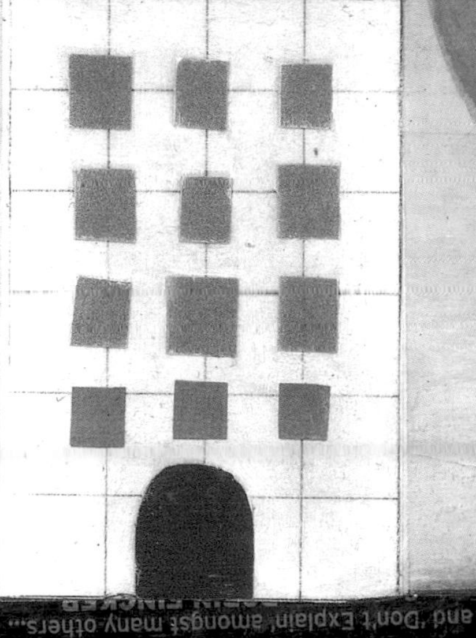

"I like to play with my friends!"

"I like my teacher.
She welcomes me with a hug."

“It’s fun to play on the slide.”

"I like to play in the ball pool."

"It's snack time!
Everybody likes snacks."

“Story time is fun!
I like storybooks.”

"It is fun to sing with friends!"

"I like to paint!"

2
10
5
9
1
4
6
3

"I want to learn numbers!"

"It is time to go home."

"Mom, I miss you, too!"